The Curious Café

Lee Aucoin, *Creative Director*
Jamey Acosta, *Senior Editor*
Heidi Fiedler, *Editor*
Produced and designed by
Denise Ryan & Associates
Illustration © Helen Poole
Rachelle Cracchiolo, *Publisher*

Teacher Created Materials
5301 Oceanus Drive
Huntington Beach, CA 92649-1030
http://www.tcmpub.com
Paperback: ISBN: 978-1-4333-5609-4
Library Binding: ISBN: 978-1-4807-1731-2
© 2014 Teacher Created Materials

Written by
Sharon Callen

Illustrated by
Helen Poole

Open 10:00 AM to 6:00 PM daily

A

Alpha Bites

10¢ per letter

Alpha Bites are our famous fruit and vegetable letters. We make all 26 letters of the alphabet. Spell any word you like. Have fun working out what your words are worth.

Try to make your name!

B

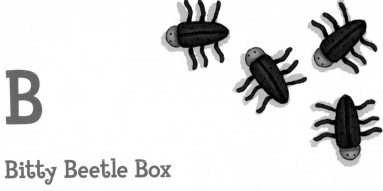

Bitty Beetle Box

$2.00 per box

The Bitty Beetle Box is filled with 10 itty-bitty cookies. Each beetle cookie comes with 6 little licorice legs. There are 60 legs in every box! Every bite is filled with creepy crawly goodness.

Yum!

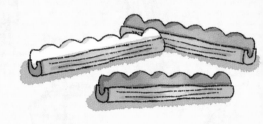

C

Crunchy Caterpillars

50¢ each

Crunchy Caterpillars are celery sticks filled with tasty fillings. Munch your way through cream cheese, peanut butter, or crazy chili-cheese caterpillars.

Save 30¢ when you order all 3.

D

Dragon-Fruit Dips

$1.00 each

Dragon-Fruit Dips are cubes, spheres, and pyramids of dragon fruit. Each one is dipped in dark chocolate. Order 6 Dragon-Fruit Dips and get 2 of each shape. Order 12 and choose how many you want of each shape!

How will you decide?

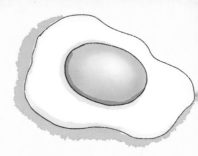

E

Eggcellent Elephant Eggs
$3.00

Wildly hungry? Order 2 extra-large eggs served on an extra-large plate! Tomato and sausage round out the meal.

Made for elephant-sized appetites!

F

Flying Fish

$1.50

Try our Flying Fish. These fish fingers are made with 4 fun fruit wings. Guess the exact weight of your fish and they're free.

Hint: They will weigh less than a pound.

G

Great Grape Shapes

$1.00 per bunch

We create Great 3-D Grape Shapes using grapes of every shape, size, and color! Choose a Great Grape Shape from our case of cubes, cones, pyramids, spheres, or cylinders.

We also supply 3-D glasses.

H

Half and Half

$2.00 per whole

Cherry or chocolate? Berry or banana? Having trouble choosing a cupcake? Why not order half of this and half of that? You'll get 2 flavors instead of 1! Buy 2 halves and have a whole lot of fun.

Share them with a friend.

I

Ice-Cream Igloos

Prices range from 90¢ to $1.25

Enjoy an icy experience eating an igloo! Ice-Cream Igloos are made from our most popular ice-cream flavors. They are served in an ice bowl to keep them icy cold. Our ice cream is kept at 0°F degrees. So it is always freezing!

3 oz. Junior Cups................ 90¢

4 oz. Just So Cups $1.10

5 oz. Jumbo Cups $1.25

The perfect treat for a hot day!

J

Juicy Jiggling Jelly

$1.00

Looking for a jolt of juice? Try our jewel-toned jelly made from pure fruit juices.

Pure fruit juice + Gelatin = Juicy Jiggling Jelly.

You'll love this wobbly treat!

K

King Kebabs

$1.50 per kebab

King Kebabs include 12 pieces of
fruit on a skewer. Choose 4 favorite
fruits. You'll get 3 pieces of each!
Then, we make your King Kebab
into a beautiful treat.

This is a real royal feast!

L

Lemon, Lime, and Lemonade

Prices range from 50¢ to $1.50

We fill a cone with scoops of ice in your choice of 5 fabulous flavors. Choose from lemon, lime, lemonade, licorice, and lavender.

1 scoop .... 50¢

2 scoops .... 90¢

3 scoops $1.20

4 scoops $1.40

5 scoops $1.50

The more scoops you buy, the less you pay!

M

Muesli Mountain

$2.00 per cup

Make your own Muesli Mountain
with our mystery muesli mix. Then,
top it off with our snow milk.
Mystery muesli mix has 3 different
types of grains, nuts, seeds, and
dried fruits.

**Find all 12 ingredients in every
Muesli Mountain.**

N

Nutty Tic Tac Toe

$2.00 per game

Nutty Tic Tac Toe comes with a playing board and your choice of nutty pieces. Choose 2 types of nuts, 1 for each player. Keep playing until you get hungry!

Make sure you don't go nuts!

O

Odds-or-Evens Omelet

$2.00 per egg

Order an Odds-or-Evens Omelet.
It will have either an odd or an
even number of eggs in it. It all
depends on how many eggs our chef
feels like cracking. You might get a
2-egg omelet. Or you could get
a 5-egg omelet!

Take a chance!

P

Porcupine Pears

Prices range from $1.00 to $2.00

A pet porcupine makes a perfect snack! Porcupine Pears are made from half a pear. Toothpick spikes are topped with plenty of pieces of peaches and pears.

Papa Porcupine: 30 toothpick spikes $2.00

Mama Porcupine: 20 toothpick spikes $1.50

Baby Porcupine: 10 toothpick spikes $1.00

Not intended for those who may be afraid of sharp objects!

19

Q

Curious Quarter Quiches

$2.00 per quarter

Our Curious Quarter Quiches are perfect for people who like solving mysteries. Each piece of quiche is different. There is one main ingredient in each quarter. Your mission is to identify it!

This will test your taste buds!

R

Rainbow Rolls

$1.75 per roll

Rainbow Rolls are made in every color of the rainbow. There's red, orange, yellow, green, blue, indigo, and violet! Fill them with rainbow jellies and jams!

Buy 7 rolls and save $1.25.

S

Super Spaghetti

$3.00 per nest

Try our super little nests of pasta.
Each nest is filled with sauce and 12
baby cheese balls.

Too cute!

T

The Taco Train

$3.50 per train

The Taco Train is made of 3 tacos filled with the tastiest taco mix in town. They're served on a long plate, with a 10-inch track of taco sauce and a cylinder of iced tea.

Choo! Choo!

23

u

Upside-Down Cupcakes

$1.50 per cupcake

The best part of a cupcake is the icing, right? So we've made these cakes upside down. Now, you can work from the bottom up! We turned the price upside down, too!

A yummy bargain!

V

Very Many Vegetable Trio

$3.00 for the trio

Order the Very Many Vegetable Trio.
You get a pizza, a shake, and a cake!

Pizza: 2 slices of mixed veggie goodness

Shake: a blend of 2 popular vegetables

Cake: 2 slices of carrot cake

Too much?

W

Watermelon Whiz

$1.00 per cylinder

The Watermelon Whiz is our own wondrous mix. It's made of 90% melon juice and 10% soda water. Visit our whizzing machine to catch your own cup of Watermelon Whiz.

Start with a scoop of ice cream and choose your favorite extras to add on top! Ordering for 2? Get a double scoop and double extras!

Gee, whiz!

X

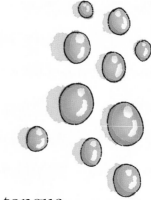

eXtra Fizz

$1.00 per glass

This drink will make your tongue tingle and your nose tickle! It's served in an eXtra tall glass with an eXtra long straw.

Fizz whiz!

Y

Yay for Yellow!

50¢ per yellow fruit

Lots of foods are yellow! So order a
Yay for Yellow Meal! Enjoy a plate
of fresh yellow foods. There are at
least a dozen yellow foods to sample.

**Want to feel mellow?
Just eat yellow!**

Z

Zebra Smoothie

$2.00

Do you like yogurt and fresh blackberries? We bet you do! We use them to make our black-and-white-striped Zebra Smoothie. Get yours within 2 minutes, or the smoothie is free! Watch the time on our digital clock!

Enjoy the matching straw!

29

Peach Tree is the chef at The Curious Café.
Peach trained at Café 1234 in Rome.

The Curious Café

2 Square Place
Sparks, Earth

Tel: 775-555-1123
Email: Peach@thecuriouscafé.com

Sharon Callen lives in Adelaide, South Australia. Sharon is a writer, a teacher, and a literacy consultant who works with children, teachers, and administrators in elementary schools. She spent a number of years working in New York City schools before returning home to Adelaide. Sharon wrote many books for Read! Explore! Imagine! Fiction Readers, including *Ms. Wilde and Oscar, Soo Yun's Book, The Happy Faces Leave Home*, and *The Lovely One*.

Helen Poole lives in Liverpool, England. Helen works digitally with an interactive pen display. She enjoys experimenting with different brush styles and textures, and creating new characters and the worlds they inhabit. Helen has worked products ranging from toys and games to magazines, greeting cards, packaging, pet products, and, of course, children's books. Helen illustrated *Footprints on the Moon*, and *Ready, Set, Go!* for Read! Explore! Imagine! Fiction Readers.